Daddy Doesn't Have to Be a Giant Anymore

Daddy Doesn't Have to Be a Giant Anymore

by JANE RESH THOMAS
Illustrated by Marcia Sewall

Clarion Books
New York

I like my daddy when he isn't acting like a giant. When he's happy, he holds me on his lap and tells me stories. He rocks me in the porch swing on hot nights when I can't sleep. We sing soft songs about the Raggedy Man and Old MacDonald. We watch the lightning bugs blinking in the dark.

If he doesn't sneak into the garage to drink whiskey, he's just Daddy. We work together in the yard on Saturday mornings. He mows the grass while I pull the weeds by the fence and notice what we need to fix.

On Saturday afternoons, Daddy and Mommy and I have picnics at the park. We swim until our lips turn blue, and then we roast some hot dogs. He helps me build the fire. "There's nothing better than a hot dog you've roasted black for me," he says, when I give him one of mine.

Usually Daddy acts as nice as pie. But I never know when he might get mad and start acting like an angry giant. This summer Mommy was mad at me every day too. After I went to bed, she yelled so much about Daddy's drinking that I couldn't sleep. Almost every night, their giant voices climbed the stairs. I lay very quiet and watched the dark shapes behind my bedroom door turn into bears and witches.

Once I found a whiskey bottle in Daddy's closet under the shoes. He stuck another bottle behind the rakes in the garage. He even hid one at the bottom of the attic stairs. Once he went to the attic and shut the door. I waited in the hall till he came out.

"What were you doing in there?" I asked.

Daddy grabbed my shoulders. "Don't snoop around and spy on me!" he said in a giant voice. When he bent down and shook me, he was bigger than a house. Bigger than a mountain. His breath smelled like the bottles I'd found.

I ran to my room and took out my dolls. I pulled off Raggedy Andy's feet.

The next morning, when Daddy was still asleep, Mommy said, "I'm sorry I've been so cranky this summer. You must be scared when Daddy and I fight."

I couldn't think of anything to say, so I looked out the window. My friends were playing hopscotch on the sidewalk.

"Dad has a problem that makes life hard for him and everybody else," she said. "Today some of the people who love him most are coming here to talk to him. We're going to tell him how we feel about his drinking."

Mommy turned my face gently with her hand and looked into my eyes. "You don't have to talk. You don't even have to stay, or listen. But I think Dad would like to know how you feel, too. If you want to tell him."

I imagined Daddy standing like a giant over me, shaking me and yelling that I shouldn't spy. My tummy ached so much I couldn't eat my cereal.

One by one, the people came. Grandma, and Daddy's friend Bob from work, and Uncle Nick all met together in our kitchen with Mommy and me. They sat around the table, talking softly and nibbling doughnuts. Mommy even let me have a sip of coffee. Grandma stopped talking in the middle of a word when we heard Daddy on the stairs.

Mommy put her arm around Daddy's waist. "Come in here with us," she said. "Have some coffee, honey." She hadn't called him "honey" for a long, long time.

He rubbed his whiskers. Then he sat down with his hands in the pockets of his bathrobe and wiggled his bare toes.

"Who's having a party?" said Daddy.

"You are," said Uncle Nick.

Daddy didn't smile. He wouldn't look at anybody's eyes.

One by one, the grownups began to talk. They told Daddy about his drinking. Uncle Nick remembered the time Daddy fell off the dock. I remembered too. He blamed me because I couldn't hold the canoe still. He shouted at me till his face turned red. Mommy hung all the dollar bills from his pockets on the clothesline to dry.

"Last time we went fishing, you snagged me in the cheek with your lure because you were drunk," said Uncle Nick. "You're my only brother. I hate to see you like that."

I began to shiver.

"That's none of your business!" Daddy said in a loud voice. He jumped up and bumped the table. Everybody's coffee spilled.

"It is my business," said Uncle Nick. "You took my little girl sailing in a storm when you were drunk."

Grandma reminded Daddy of the time he knocked her birthday cake off the table. She hadn't even blown the candles out. Grandma cried at her own birthday party. Her dog Buddy was the only happy one there. He licked the frosting off the rug.

"We love you. Get some doctoring, for goodness' sake," Grandma said to Daddy in a shaky voice.

Daddy glared at Grandma. "I don't need doctors. I just drink a little to relax, like everybody else."

I wrapped my bathrobe tighter. When would they call on me?

"You miss a day of work almost every week because you're drunk," said Bob. "Yesterday you snarled at a customer. I've always liked you, but I'm going to have to let you go."

"That's ridiculous!" Daddy looked as though he couldn't believe Bob had said such things. "Would you really fire me?"

"You used to be my best worker, but now the other guys complain because you don't do your share."

I didn't like to hear Bob complain about my daddy. But I remembered times when he didn't get up for work. Once last winter Mommy got mad at him. She pulled the covers off the bed and opened the window. The snow blew in on Daddy's bare feet. He yelled at Mommy in his giant voice and yanked the blankets back. Then he slept till lunchtime.

I put my hands over my face and watched the grownups between my fingers. What would happen to me if Daddy lost his job?

Now it was Mommy's turn. She talked about the camping trip when Daddy sneaked whiskey in his tackle box and his backpack and got too drunk to put up the tent. She told about the time he drove me home from school when he was drunk. We almost skidded into the ditch.

"I can't stand it anymore!" said Mommy. And then she talked in a voice so soft I could hardly hear. "I love you, and I can't live with your drinking. I've talked with people at the hospital. Either you go there for treatment, or I leave."

Daddy slammed his coffee cup on the table. "I can stop drinking anytime I want to!"

Then everybody turned and looked at me. I opened my mouth, but no words came out. Where would Mommy live, if she didn't live with Daddy? Would she take me with her? I felt as small as an ant. What could I tell him? He might get mad enough to shake me again.

But he didn't seem mad. Instead, he knelt beside my chair and whispered, "What do you think?"

"You scare me when you shout and shake me," I whispered back.

He hugged me with a soft Daddy hug. "I want you to rock me on the front porch and count the lightning bugs and sing in the dark," I said in his ear.

He sat down in his chair again and put his head in his hands. He looked too tired to sit up straight. Nobody said anything for a long time.

Then Daddy stared at Mommy. "I need some time to think," he said. He went down the basement. We could hear him pounding nails. All the visitors went home, whispering their good-byes to us as they left. The house was still for a long time.

At last Daddy climbed the stairs with slow steps. "I'll go for treatment," he told Mommy. "Would you help me pack my stuff?"

Mommy and I followed Daddy and watched him pack his suitcase. He put his toothbrush and his razor in the little leather kit and sat down on the bed. Mommy folded his underwear and patted his socks as if they were alive. She sat down beside him.

I hugged my teddy bear and didn't say a word.

"Do you think it's your fault I'm going away?" said Daddy.

Teddy nodded for me.

"You only made me brave enough to go," said Daddy.

"You can borrow Teddy to hold you in the dark," I said.

We all hugged each other, with Teddy in the middle.

Daddy was gone for a long time. We ate five Sunday dinners without him. Five Saturdays I watched cartoons while Mommy did the crossword puzzle. For old times' sake, she said, because Daddy wasn't there to do it.

Mommy stopped being crabby all the time. Nobody yelled after I went to bed, and she bought me a nightlight. "Now you can see all the shadows aren't bears and witches," she said, "but only your ratty old bathrobe." She and I sewed Raggedy Andy's feet back on.

Mommy and I walked to the lake after supper every night, even when it rained. We swam together inside the ropes, while the lifeguard watched us from his tower to make sure we were safe. Sometimes we skipped all the way home.

Laughing, he picked me up and whirled me around in the good old way. Mommy went into the house.

"Are you a little scared of me?" Daddy asked.

I nodded.

"It's mostly the whiskey that makes me scary, and I hope that's over. I'm trying my best," he said. "Now I have a job to do. Would you like to help?"

He and I collected all the bottles he had hidden. Some were in places I hadn't found. He poured the whiskey down the sink and put the bottles in the trash. There was a whole bag full.

"It won't be easy to stay sober," Daddy said. "But I'm working on it every day. I don't want to be scary anymore."

Tonight Daddy rocked me in the dark and sang the good old songs. "Let's count the fireflies' taillights," he said. We counted twenty-three.

Tomorrow, after we mow the lawn and trim the weeds by the fence, Mommy and Daddy and I are going to have a picnic at the lake.

We'll swim until our lips are blue, and then we'll build a fire for the hot dogs. I'll roast one black for Daddy, just the way he likes them.

To Nancy Coleman
— J.R.T.

Clarion Books
a Houghton Mifflin Company imprint
215 Park Avenue South, New York, NY 10003
Text copyright © 1996 by Jane Resh Thomas
Illustrations copyright © 1996 by Marcia Sewall
Illustrations executed in pen and ink, watercolor, and pastel
on Fabriano cold-press paper.
Type is 13/19 Sabon
Book design by Carol Goldenberg

For information about this and other Houghton Mifflin trade and refer-
ence books and multimedia products, visit The Bookstore at Houghton
Mifflin on the World Wide Web at (http://www.hmco.com/trade/).
Printed in Singapore.

Library of Congress Cataloging-in-Publication Data
Thomas, Jane Resh.
Daddy doesn't have to be a giant anymore / by Jane Resh Thomas ;
illustrated by Marcia Sewall.
p. cm.
Summary: A little girl is frightened of her daddy when he's drunk,
but with the support of his family and friends he enters a
treatment program and resolves to stay sober.
ISBN 0-395-69427-2
[1. Alcoholism—Fiction. 2. Fathers and daughters—Fiction.
3. Family Life—Fiction.] I. Sewall, Marcia, ill. II. Title.
PZ7.T36695Dad 1996
[E]—dc20   94-24511
CIP   AC
TWP   10 9 8 7 6 5 4 3 2 1